The Twentieth Century Epic

Reuben Brodie Garnett

Alpha Editions

This edition published in 2024

ISBN : 9789362517265

Design and Setting By
Alpha Editions
www.alphaedis.com
Email - info@alphaedis.com

As per information held with us this book is in Public Domain.
This book is a reproduction of an important historical work. Alpha Editions uses the best technology to reproduce historical work in the same manner it was first published to preserve its original nature. Any marks or number seen are left intentionally to preserve its true form.

Preface

By the Author.

This poem that I have dignified with the term epic, was written by inspiration, and is dedicated to the human race. I have used the term epic with no intention of assuming a dignity not due my production; but, in the sense that the precepts and warnings contained therein, have a lofty purpose; and are graphically set forth in the plainest words in the English language.

I have not indulged in similes or hyperboles; nor does my epic abound with those picturesque figures of comparison found in Homer or Virgil, nor those cadences and swells found in The Paradise Lost, describing the headlong falls and gigantic flights of those god-like personages peopling the heavens and earth in the poetic mind; nor does my inspiration come from muse or divine breath; nor did it descend upon me from above; on the contrary, it sprang up out of the deep feeling I have for my kind, especially those in the strained walks of life.

Our twentieth century shows society in the process of centralizing itself; and, gradually forcing us into legal socialism. Thisis plainly shown in the poem. The process of centralization, for years, worked slowly in this country. As long as the influence of the founders of our Republic was potent, liberty was dominant.

The first step in this process was the inauguration of a general system of free public schools. The direct result of this free education was to overcrowd the book and head portion of our population at the expense of the producing classes, making it harder for the clerk to make a bare living. The idea of every parent now seems to be that his or her offspring is especially adapted to the learned professions and to society.

This was also the first step towards the diversion of public funds to private enterprise. The appropriation of public moneys to the extensive and widening fields of private affairs has progressed rapidly in the last decade. This, with its evils, is vividly set forth in my poem. Unless this is checked by united, immediate action, socialism will increase more rapidly in the future than in the past, is my prophecy. This results from the fact that the tax-eaters are the ones who manipulate our bond elections.

The result is plain, and can be predicted with certainty; the end of socialism will be the extreme opposite and, that you all knowis anarchy. When everything is so striking that nothing strikes, or in other words, when there are more laws than we can possibly tolerate, we'll naturally rebel and kick them all over; all, as shown in this epic. The last transition will likely be accomplished by bloodshed and strife.

The laws for the management of society in a state of complete legal socialism will be so numerous and complicated; and the bureaus so haughty and domineering that freemen will not try to learn them, much less obey them. In fact, no one can now keep pace with the rapid production of laws under our incipient socialism. The fight I make is to break off now and go back to fundamentals, as shown in my poem.

As against socialism or anarchy I deliberately prefer the latter; but, as against both of them I prefer a government of limited powers, based exclusively on natural laws that I have so forcibly defined in this work; with a complete abandonment of the barbarous idea of punishment for crimes by criminal courts; the man who commits a crime is to be pitied and helped to a more sane mode of existence, and not be driven into perpetual criminality. As to how he shall be handled can be better settled when we clear ourselves of our false notions on the subject.

Our legal servants, we call officers, are now deteriorating with great rapidity, as set forth in this poem under "Names." My remedy for that is to cut down the salaries of all officers from President down, so low that no one will seek office for money. Then have the laws such that men will be selected and compelled to serve, by public sentiment, for short terms and take out part of their pay in patriotism and good will.

My observation, over a number of years, shows that the higher the salary, the more inefficient the officer. High salaries also give birth to gangs of politicians who fatten off the public funds and salaries of their appointees, making graft semi-respectable.

Honesty in public and private life seems to me to be very desirable; and, it could be so easily attained, as set forth in my epic. Of course, under our prevailing system, honesty is out of the question; and if any of you think that I have not convicted you of dishonesty, as defined under that topic, please send me your photograph to be used herein.

In writing this poem I have no malice in my heart for a single human being on earth; and, if in any way I have touched upon any of your pet notions or sacred ideas, and thereby wounded your feelings,I sincerely ask your forgiveness; with me all truth is sacred. I have no ill-will against preachers, lawyers, or doctors; I wrote you up to make you think, and also to let you know you were not fooling me.

In conclusion, I say to you one and all, as brothers and fellow citizens, let's work together to save the greatest country and the greatest civilization on earth.

Let truth together bind us,
And supporting it find us.

REUBEN BRODIE GARNETT.

June 29, 1913.

Proem

I never shall appeal to any muse of old
To give inspiration to my story when it's told,
But, in words all my own, shall my theme unfold;
And, for my love of man, I'll tell you what I can;
Tell you what I know that you may truly scan
What to do and what to know for the good of man;
Tell you where to go, the places you should shun
On every working day, when your labor's done.
In telling where to go I will not name the place
Where you should show your face, but let each run his race
And, for himself decide the spot to cast his lot.
I'll point out mistakes to help put on brakes
Against the evils of our day one often makes.
From the Charlatan and all designing wise
Strip his robe of guise and expose him to your eyes.
The fawning sycophant and all his crafty kind
Will be painted so they'll not be hard to find.

I'll speak of laws and customs old with hoary age
Taught by rulers, priests, and many an ancient sage
That now are practically extinct with non-usage;
And regulations new that men had little to do
With bribes sometimes when they put them through
Legislative halls and Congress we'd now eschew.
I'll speak to you about your manners
When you sometimes march with banners;
And even with hosannas sitting meekly in your pew

Revolving schemes against others you intend to do.
The roving politicians all seeking fat positions
To feed their hungry maws and all their kin-in-laws
Come in for their share when we divide the flaws.
Even the society genteel in their swift automobile
Had better beware their piccadillos to conceal.
Religions of every shade by ancients and moderns made
To subdue the gentle folk with all that they have said
This subject will meet its due before I'm through,
As I started out for things about that need review.
Theatres too, with music, painting and art,
Might all feel slighted not to have their part
In the criticism we bring as they my song may sing;
And the pictures my word recalls may be carved on walls
In the coming days as was done with other poet's lays.
Developments in science where we place reliance
To alleviate the misdirection of our state
Should all be alluded to in the story we relate.
Wars, with all their frightful havoc spread
Where victorious and routed passed over dying and dead,
And peace too that came at last
That o'er the earth its healing blessings amassed
Should have a place when in plates my work is cast;
Also ethics, that practical theme so misunderstood,
Should here be elucidated for the general good;
And a few short digressions would not be out of place

In an Epic dedicated to and written for The Human Race.

But what is said under each head you may read,
So to my task the work shall proceed.

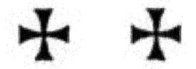

✢ ✢

Admonition

Take from your statute laws and books
All legal protection for thieves and crooks;
Your complicated bills of mechanics' liens
That offer to rogues the ample means
The owners of houses with their demesnes
To make go down humbly into their jeans
For the jingly coin doubly to pay
The working man, and padded expenses defray.
Your unjust schemes of municipal taxation
That cause home owners such great vexation.
Your tax upon mortgages, bills and notes
Upon which the poor man's title barely floats,
Causing him to pay levies upon his lands
As if they were clear like the rich man's;
By increasing for him his interest and dues
Which the money sharks collect as they choose.

Your laws against usury one may take
Tend solely the poor man's back to break.
You drive away the cheap money he might get,
And leave him at the mercy of that lawless set
Who fatten upon unfortunates suddenly thrown in debt.
Nearly all your laws for the collection of dues
Into our commercial life dishonesty infuse.
Your regulations of homestead, exemption and stay
Simply postpone our troubles to another day.
By intricate trials with their writs and pleas;
And copious objections about titles and fees,

Remainders absolute, contingent and entailed,
Upon technicalities numberless justice is impaled;
Your instructions, your errors and appeals,
Until the waiting, anxious litigant feels
That the door of the temple of justice is locked;
And his chance of right is securely blocked.
Your free legal aid and your festive welfare board,
Their matrons and clerks, a mighty hungry hoard,

Impose upon the payers of taxes a weighty load;
All for the purpose of sending over the road
Some unfortunate victim of their own slimy graft
Or some poor devil whom they kick "fore and aft."
Your Juvenile court of which the kids make sport,
Where curtailed haired women and men hold the fort.
And such institutions the wits of man can devise
Are considered by Progressives as blessings in disguise.
Your tariffs for protection passed in Congress halls
To build all around us mighty Chinese walls,
Are sapping from the people their dear blood of life,
And making for politicians no end of deadly strife.
Your proctor with his aids to fight against divorce;
Who by his pugnacity is seeking to enforce
Unfortunate couples bound in unhappy wedded lock
To parade their troubles upon the public dock;
And to bind the chains anew they seek to dissever,

Holding them fast that he may be deemed clever,
In the estimation of all the Christian Endeavor;

And that class of persons who want now and forever
To meddle in the affairs of all whomsoever
Are not able to disclaim the care they obtain;
Who crowd upon the weak the blessings they do not seek;
All to achieve for themselves a home in the sky
When from their missions on earth they fly.
The Commissioners of Vice are pulling for a slice
Of fame as it goes by investigating those
Who employ many girls simply to keep them in hose
And such other fancy articles that they suppose
Will always make them shine when they go out to dine,
As a girl dressed up haply feels fine.
And now here comes Teddy with his big stick and hat
For damages to his soiled name in legal spat,
With a small newspaper man suing for a big chunk

Because he published that T. R. had been drunk.
To tell the names of men who are shams in our times
Would overload my epic with variegated rhymes:
The one named above is more than a man;
He stands for ideas, a party and a clan
Born of disappointment and just turned loose
Sailing under the banner of the Big Bull Moose.
This clique of theirs all swelling up to burst
Decry all our institutions to be the very worst.
They'd have our laws, judges and courts recalled,
And others to suit them forthwith installed.
They'd regulate the wages men have to pay,
Neglecting to tell the laborer he might be in the way

Unless his work he did should his employers pay;
For unless his production his pay did compensate
He and others would soon be off the slate.
They told us too in tones as loud as they could prate
How all the monied men and trusts they'd regulate,
Carefully hiding the man who was running their slate,

And supplying the funds for them to navigate.
The working man too his dinner pail they'd fill
Forgetting also to tell him to send in his bill.
They'd secure to all the women free right to vote,
So they could say to hubby: "We've got your goat."
And volumes of such ideas upon us did they float
All too numerous in this article to quote.
Drop your silly custom not worn off by growth
That judicial bodies must put a witness to oath,
That all he says and all that he shall quote
Will be the truth and nothing but the truth,
About the matters he relates in his witness booth.
The reasons for this habit have long passed forsooth,
It deceives none on bench or in jury box;
It may occasionally aid some old, designing fox
To some youthful, verdant judge deceive
And, of some just debt himself relieve.
On the whole, it does more harm than good
As at present the thing is generally understood:

For in a contested suit with one who knows
Against a trembly one who partially shows

Some lingering faith in "Old Scare Crows,"
The inclination to lie and deceive in the one
Would surely be by the other simply outdone:
The one might be bound by the fears of hell
While the other swears away his lies to tell.
When the witness swears he's perjured unawares,
For by his plight he must the whole truth reveal
By the rule he must more than half conceal.
Stop your fight for prohibition and do the fair thing;
Our people to temperance themselves will shortly bring.
Take taxes off whisky, wine, liquor and beer;
And, for the cause of temperance you needn't have a fear.
Let all your marts and markets freely sell
Every kind of liquor they ever heard tell;
Let every one the stuff make from gulf to lake;
Make the price so cheap that with one leap,
Men will forsake the common thing to keep.
At one cent a drink the bar keeper will think
His saloon will sink and soon put him on the brink

Of finding some other way all his expenses to pay;
So out soon he goes not stopping his doors to close.
There still will be drinking and that keeps you thinking,
That by compulsion you can create a revulsion
In the taste of man heap sooner than you can.
The truth is, you've always tried in vain
All these cultivated tastes of man to restrain.
The more you try to force men good habits to acquire,
The more you stir up and increase his raging desire,

To show his freedom against which you conspire.
He'll go to any extent which you'll never prevent,
To get his booze on which his mind is bent;
He'll keep his "blind tigers" and his wooden legs,
Hollowed out and neatly made with faucet of pegs,
His whisky he'll conceal and feel he's in the right;
So you'll not stop him no matter how you fight.
The drunkard will drink no matter what you think,

At any cost no matter if you consider him lost.
Make the price so cheap that for his family's keep,
He'll still be ahead to buy his folks their bread.

✠ ✠

A Digression

I used to tell my friends what I was going to do,

And right away they'd say, "I wouldn't if I were you."

I know of once or twice by taking their advice,

A good deal I lost at a distressing cost.

Take my advice; choose your own course to pursue,

And, when you get your plan, just put it through,

And then tell no other man what you've been up to.

Then if you succeed you will never need,

Anybody else to claim part of your deed.

Even if you fail, don't furl up your sail

Nor put your head under the bottom rail,

But try once more just the same as before.

Dorothy

Dorothy

Listen to this story about a little girl,
Who came into the world a short time ago.
I remember the day, only a few months or so;
It was in the month of March over a year;
When all trembling with hope and fear,
We did for her watch—all sincere.
At night she came, and without any name,
Because we did not know what her sex would be;
But at her scream, the doctor said "she";
And, then, we all at once knew what to do;
About naming her the course to pursue.
We left it to her mother, herself a little bride,
This weighty matter of naming all to decide.
We told her all the names we did hear or see,
But she rejected them all and called her Dorothy.
So Dorothy's my theme her grandmother's dream,
During all those years when those babes of hers,
Us did come to see, and, now she still avers,
That she watched through the passing years
Looking to see if one of hers a girl might be,

But they were boys, the whole blessed three.
Now Dorothy's here to fill our home with cheer
By her little, prattling talk and her shambling walk,
By her little tricks she plays in her winning ways,
Pulling off your hat and fumbling your cravat,
Knocking over chairs, trying to go upstairs,
Picking all the flowers for grandpa to smell,

And more other things than tongue or pen can tell.
She's a little sprite and good for our sight.
But here I must pause and sadly say,
That one evil day a swelling came on her neck,
We thought for sure had come from us to take
The little brat, and all our hearts to break.
But the good doctor came and now she's the same
As she was before the blasted swelling came.
May I never see the day till my race on earth is run
When any evil at all shall befall this little one.
Many of you have plenty of such chaps,
That jump up and down upon your laps,

Who are just as pretty and just as sweet;
And you walk with them upon the street,
To the market and to the drug store,
Where you buy food stuffs for them galore,
Just the same as I do for mine o'er and o'er.
But still with me a great difference I see,
Between your brats and my Dorothy,
And the reason that you do not with me agree
Is simply because you are you and I am me.

☩ ☩

Divorce

Now drop a little tear, but don't stop here,
Come along now and let's see if we can agree
Upon another matter while o'er the thing I scatter
Some thoughts I have, not intending myself to flatter.
Divorce is a question about which many disagree;
Some think it's wrong; some think it's right maybe.
Now upon it let's begin our wordy fight and see.
For a beginning I will postulate, simply to open the debate,

That it is not an affair of the state that couples separate,
When they each other fervently hate;
Except where children, a care about whose fate,
On the conscience of the public might grate,
Are brought into court for the judge to state
In his judicial opinion of the case,
What he considers best for the human race.
Then of course if His Honor is wise, he'll devise
Some plan to make wife and man either realize,
That if they are deaf to the cries of their offspring
The court itself will bring pressure into the thing
They're about to do, and, before it gets through,
I think that neither me nor you will any suggestion make
Or advice give about what course the law will take.
If when all this is done and the court can't make them one,
Then it is up to him and all my talk is done.
Some people oppose divorce on account of their views,
Acquired from that book written by ancient Jews.

Some think it a disgrace upon the entire human race,
For any sundered couples to have a place,
On the green earth where they may show their face.
This narrow view is not entertained by you or me,
Because we've been along far enough to see
Some of the things from whom some are set free.
Others oppose it on the score of "I told you so!
People oughtn't marry whom they did not know."
Some plunge deep into the matter, themselves they flatter,
That they can some great big principles scatter,
Over the very causes while they chatter.
They'd take it in time and let the big state
Issue its own red-sealed certificate,
To all spooning couples longing to mate,
And, at one single throw the entire nuisance abate.
Then these smart ones pucker their mouth,
With their heads tossed north and south,
To see if anybody should really act so shoddy,
As not an acquiescent head to at once noddy.
But the main fight does not come from home,

It thunders from the pope of Rome;
And, there are plenty of folks take his word home.
He says marriage is the sacred thing of life,
And when one takes a wife, regardless of strife,
They cannot be cut apart with a butcher's knife.
So you may shake this subject up and down,
In country, village and town, and use every noun,
Verb, adverb and pronoun from early morn to sundown,

And the people will no better be made, for all your
Prattle and all you said.
The real causes of the thing are ingrain,
Born in the heart and born in the brain,
Maybe, by any by, before you die, but not I,
Science may teach us to create and the race propagate,
In some other way besides this vexing marriage state.

Social Evil

The next subject allied the last, on to which
I have been trying my train of thoughts to switch,
Is one to which a common word is applied,
That just as well fits many other things beside;
But the meaning of which comes easily when tried;
And seems to pop into your heads with no upheaval,
Is that natural crime called "the social evil."
Now, I did not make people and neither did you,
But if a certain inspired book be true,
Some one made man for a start,
And then chopped out him a piece near his heart,
And constructed another of a little different sort.
If this be true the "some one" must be divinity
For, ever since, there has been a mysterious affinity,
Between the two kinds in every community.
On this subject we must not too widely roam,
Because it might bring some trouble home,
To some of you married men who every now and then

Feel like jumping out of your own pen.
Legislation and investigation and even humiliation,
Over all creation, in homes of every station,
Among peoples of every tribe and nation,
Have to this offense brought emancipation.
Women have been burned at the stake,
In attempting to make them forsake,
The lives they were leading, the men they were bleeding.
In all your statute books, in corners and nooks,

Laws have been framed against every thing that looks
Towards countenancing any form of prostitution:
Yet with all this and your contribution,
In your vain attempts to revise the constitution
Of woman and man ever since the world began,
You have not yet laid the foundation
For killing this wicked institution.
You have tried segregation into dark streets,
Where your own policemen lose their beats;
You have tried fines in the police courts,
Where they fetch up all the regular sports;
You have even gone yourself among the slums;
And feigned to be treating them as your chums,

Doing your levelest to put them under your thumbs,
And yet this evil does not seem to succumb;
Now what can we do but to stop trying,
And to our several good wives lying
About where we've been now and then.
You let this subject alone and stay at home
As much as you can for the good of man.
The more you talk and act wise,
The more you'll advertise the thing to eyes
That see and ears that hear
When you think no eavesdropper is near.

✠ ✠

Woman Suffrage

As my train of thought rumbled over the
Last topic it nearly tumbled;
And, metre, I see, was hard to gee:
But the subject next calling for my attention,
Has me so perplexed that I scarcely can mention
Even the little that I know and the facts show
About woman suffrage more than you already know.
Because I once rode with Phoebe Cousins
And have read suffrage pieces by dozens;

I've even heard Susan B. at the time that she
Her speeches did make our customs to break,
And yet, with all of that, little is under my hat,
To enlighten you or tell you where I'm at
Upon this subject great where women of late
Their rights to get are defying the state.
In Old Great Britt'n many of 'em are sitt'n
Starving in jails sooner than lower their sails.
But, considering it all, it looks to me,
That if you make your ballots universally free
To every living man who on top of earth walks
And to every single, solitary woman who talks
You wouldn't help us much to get us out of the clutch
Of bad laws passed and the evil designing of such
As our liberties would take to—beat the Dutch.

Honesty

If in all your acquaintance, you know an honest man,
Produce him and introduce him to me if you can,
That I may get the likeness of his face
To emboss in gold for a model to the human race;
In my epic I'll give him a prominent place.
Now, don't get miffed at me, till my meaning you see
And my definition you fully understand of honesty.
I can find plenty of people anywhere
Who will not lie like a tiger in his lair,
Ready to pounce upon you, your neck to break,
Your horse to steal and your watch to take;
Who will not break into your house at night,
And commit burglary without any light;
Or in your pocket slip his slimy hands
To snake out your money where he stands;
Or who will not murder, rob and plunder
Or steal your child your roof from under;
Or who will not commit any of your crimes
And pay all that they owe, even to dimes
And contracts keep square within the lines;
And yet none of these come up you see,
To my idea of what true honesty must be.

Now an honest man will strictly follow facts
In every thing he thinks, believes, or acts;
When he knows the truth that will guide his way.
Where there are no winding paths for him to stray.
He will not suppress the evidence in a case,

Where some gain may come to him in his race
For gold, ambition, pride, or even grace.
Without uttering a word, the biggest lie ever heard,
May fly out with wings of the fleetest bird,
And in its wake its venom shake over our heads,
Bringing distress and grief its desolation sheds.
By simple look, wink, or nod of the head,
We give assent to whatever is said;
And in that way push falsehood straight ahead.
Nothing at all may be asked, no inquiry made,
Still we should tell about the horse we trade;
If any faults he have, ring bone, spavin joint,
Pole evil, swinny or any other weak point,
We should spit it out right away
And not wait for the other fellow to say.

If a house you have to sell where one must dwell,
Tell about the plumbing and everything as well,
That makes your house unsuited to him you'd sell.
If pastor of some orthodox church you may be;
And find things in the Bible that can't agree
With reason and sense, don't get upon your knee
And pray grace to help you see that two equals three.
Speak the truth, lose your job and stay free.
When you go upon the street and a stranger meet
Who seems to know you, don't be so sweet,
And claim to know his face while you greet.
When dressed up in your only Sunday suit
That some one admires, don't begin to hoot

That it is only your old every-day suit.
When asked a simple question you cannot answer
Don't say that you've just forgot and be a romancer,
Come out with the truth, say you don't know.
When inquiry is made as to what church you go,

If you don't go to any, just say so;
Don't pretend that you go to different ones
"You know."
If you're running a bank and get short on cash
Where to extend accommodation might cause a smash,
Don't squint your goggled eyes and look wise,
And claim that you're moving the crop, otherwise,
You'd be too glad to take a loan of that size.
When you are specially invited to play or sing,
And are pining to hear your own piano ring
Don't say that you're out of practice here of late,
When you've done nothing but practice for that date.
If some one cordially asks you to have a drink,
Don't tell him that you, yourself, was on the brink
Of inviting him with you in a social glass to link.
When you have old clothes lying on the floor
That you are about to hand over to the poor,
Don't pretend that you've them simply outgrown,

When in the rag-bag they've actually been thrown.
When some dear friend implores you for a ten
Don't pull your coin case where money had been,
As if he didn't know where your full bill book stayed,

In your hip pocket crammed, the bills nicely laid.
When in your swift automobile you ride,
Don't ask any one to sit by your side,
Ride by yourself and flatter your pride,
That everybody's observing how slick you glide.
When you get on your new spring hat and green cravat,
Don't break your back trying to be so straight,
But let modesty all your demeanor regulate.
Don't feel so grand, and swagger as you go
Forgetting to whom for those things you owe.
You are dishonest in the way you treat your wife;
You go to clubs and revel in high life;
You smoke, chew and drink to your full,
While she stays at home the baby buggy to pull.
You go outing and have a jolly time;
And, when you start out, you flip her a dime;

When you do hand out a ten her things to buy,
You pull it out slow and heave a deep sigh,
And before you leave you almost make her cry,
Saying so very much about hard times being nigh;
If you ever spend a dollar freely in your life
Let it be the dollar you deliver to your wife.
Sling it out and say, "Money grows on trees!"
If she wants more you'll dash it to the breeze.
You don't always tell your wife where you've been,
And I don't advise you to, for I don't begin
To tell mine all the places where I go
And the reasons for which I'll never show.

You are dishonest in listing for your tax,
In giving in notes and bonds hid away in cracks;
And the value of your things you put so low
That when th' assessor's gone you don't know
Where you'll get your next meal, so poor you feel.
When you take your seat on the witness stool,
And swallow that solemn oath under the court rule,
The things that help your case, your lawyer told,

In your memory seem to stay with an iron hold;
But those circumstances that against you militate
Appear entirely faded off your memory plate.
A falsehood acted, spoken, thought or believed
Seems justifiable when the one by it deceived
Had no right to elicit the truth from you,
And with the matter in dispute had nothing to do;
But was merely intermeddling, taking in the view
Of people's affairs to glut his curious mind
And get into trouble if the same he'd find.
Of all the animals on earth we find anywhere
Man's the only dishonest one I do declare,
Unless the fox be called dishonest when to lead
The howling pack off his track, he runs at full speed,
And turns around and comes back over the same track
And then quickly darts off somewhere to hide,
While the hounds on the old straight track relied,
And bound ahead beyond where the fox turned back,

Thinking he's gone on and thus lose the track.

This clever deceit is accomplished so neat,
By the sly little fox who is hard to beat.
You may take the meanest horse any day,
While munching away on his bale of hay,
And he'll kick, bite, and run all the others away,
Until he gets his belly full, when he leaves
And lets the others eat the rest of the sheaves;
And doesn't lock them up in a safety deposit box.
When a man's wants are supplied, he locks
Up from all others the things he cannot use,
If he lived a thousand years his stomach to abuse.
Civilization made us dishonest, nature never did;
Deceit comes from cultivation and we'll never rid
Ourselves from its blighting evils till we undo
Many of our laws and customs made and passed by you.
Man could be made honest in a very few years,
If he could be held respectable among his peers;
But if one of us should get honest all at once,

We'd be hauled up for being a dunce;
And, an inquisition had to ascertain whether we're mad.
Our behavior would to others seem so queer,
That they would flee from us in bodily fear.
So we will have to let reformation work slow,
Until the full meaning of my epic you know.

✠ ✠

Jim Saltenstall

(A Digression.)

A certain man, stout and medium tall
Dwelt near us once, named Jim Saltenstall.
The most peculiar thing about this man,
Was not his name nor distended span.
A powerful limb was he of the law,
In which he exercised his massive jaw,
In justice courts if chance he saw,
To display his wit or pick a flaw,
In some contention neighbors hate,
Where he was ready and never too late,
To get a V for his windy prate.
A farm beside, where he did reside,
Claimed his skill and special pride.
He handled stock and rode his nag,
And had many things about which to brag.
In cows and swine his money he stuck

To raise for profit and keep him up.
The clothes he wore hung on him loose,
Except when he did faultlessly spruce
Before his friends and neighbors to strut
In court, to pull his client out of a rut.
He had one pair of extra sized pants,
Made by a cousin or one of his aunts,
Known all around by every girl and boy,
In his vicinity, made of brown corduroy.
This pair loose he'd usually wear

With no chance for the brush to tear.
One sultry afternoon in the middle of June,
A couple of spinsters riding along soon
Discovered on one side of the road
This pair of pants where it was "throwed."
As they drew up close to the spot
Their nag whirled around in a trot;
The pants were moving and jumping about
These maids their wits scaring half out.
No James was by them seen at all,
But they knew the trousers of Saltenstall,
Who had hid in weeds with none on at all.
This mystery to them riding in the lane,
He never appeared and offered to explain.
Weeks passed by before they laid eye
Upon Saltenstall for whom they did spy,
This vision and its meaning to reveal.
They imagined they heard pigs squeal,
So by ifs and whats and twisting twigs,
They guessed the pants were full of pigs.
This story is true, and the riddle plain:

James found in his pasture near the lane,
That his favorite sow the stork had blessed,
With a litter of pigs, so he was distressed,
To contrive a scheme to take pigs to barn,
And have them housed and shielded from harm.
No sack had he in which to fetch the pigs,
So these pants were used with his rigs.

When on his shoulders his pigs he did load,
In plain view he saw the maids in the road.
They were coming straight ahead in full view,
So off his shoulders the whole thing he threw,
And took to the weeds to get out of view.
These ladies came along, all as we have said,
And found matters as stated under this head.

✠ ✠

Science

We do not mean by the title above,
Christian Science, which so many love;
And, against which we have no thought to inveigh,
Because it is accomplishing some good in its day,
By teaching us to see that the power of the mind

Controls our bodies more than others find.
By science, we mean all knowledge gained
From whatever source it may be attained;
By inventions, laws, medicine, therapeutics,
Sociology, geology, astronomy, epizootics,
Geography, orthography, mentality, logics,
Government, devilment, war and fratricide;
And this list might be multiplied if we tried.
But of all those things we cannot make review.
For ages men did not know that the earth was round;
It was supposed to flat, and all the ground
Rested on the back of one man, whose picture is found
Still in old geographies, standing under his load,
With his feet upon the back of some large toad,
Or tortoise; and, that the sun was slipped clean
Back west to east, at night by us unseen,
In the chariot of the Sun-god with his team
Of steeds as swift as if they were run by steam.
These views by them held sacred were impressed
On others who even speculatively guessed,
That there might be error in the sacred book,
Or else those who read failed to look

Deep enough into lines between lines,
Where sometimes most information one finds.
Shaking off their fear, daring men began to peer,
Into the upper air with telescopes, far and near;
Until upon them dawned beyond escape,
By the picture on the moon and its shape,
That, book or no book, the world was a globe.
And, to fully prove it, they toiled and strove,
Till Columbus the Great, did daringly navigate
Far enough to see it and stop the debate.
That one hazardous stroke by this brave man
Struck the shackles from science and began
A new era, in which truth conquers belief,
And consecrated error dies to our relief.
The door now being thrown open wide, men pried,
And delved into nature with rapid stride.
By the light of astronomy as their guide,
It was discovered that those specks that shine
High up in the heavens at the night time
Are suns and worlds that in their orbits move
Around greater centers in distance so high
As not to be seen as when through glass we spy.

That all those moving worlds by one supreme law
Of gravitation yield their obedience in awe.
To the bottom of the sea men dived to find
The wrecks of ages there accumulated by time,
As old ocean waves roll over them its slime.

Into the strata of the rocks marking each age
As time passed written on them page by page,
The history of the earth before the historic age;
Men have dug up fossils for scholar and sage.
With silken thread, they drew lightning from the sky,
And harnessed it up our trade and commerce to ply.
By microscope and tools chemists use,
The varied elements have been made to fuse
Into numerous new substances by man used
In the varied arts to which existence imparts
The glories of the times from which we start.
The doctor, with his scalpel and his knife,
Discovers new means for preserving human life.
The inventor with his machines, human labor to supply,

To the plowman who plods on his weary way;
To the weaver who with his hands from day to day,
His cloth he did weave in the old-fashioned way.
The builder with his bricks of sand and clay
Once made with mud securely encased in hay
His stone, plaster, lumber, hardware and nails,
All made by machinery which little labor entails.
The merchant with his cargo laden in a ship,
Propelled by steam as over the deep they slip.
The baker with his ovens and pans,
Bakes and makes his bread without hands.
All these with telegraph and telephones supplied,
Carrying messages as over wires they slide,
With lightning speed, bringing to each his need,

Shortening time and obliterating space,
As each against the other runs his race,
For gains in the occupations they chase.
The grave lawyer sitting wise at his desk,
Dictating to stenographers things he may suggest,
About cases in court or making a report,

Of some opinion great in matters of weight
About all the business to which they relate
In the matters and things of those who wait
Their troubles to tell and business to state.
The iron horse on tracks of belted steel,
With throttle and valve, and whistle peal
Rolling over the land, propelled by steam,
Crossing mountain, valley and stream,
On tracks, rails and bridges of steel.
The flying machine shot up in mid air
Sailing over continents in feats they dare,
Rivaling the plumed eagle in his flight,
Or those swift birds that pass in a night,
From out their abodes beyond human sight.
The magic needle that points to the pole,
Guiding navigation on oceans untold;
And those brave adventurers seeking the pole,
Where the earth on its axis turns,
To find that for which their ambition burns:
Losing their crew in the cold, wintry snow,
Too weak from hunger, them to follow.
And onward, how far can the genius of man go?

With Edison, the wizard, putting on a show
Of actors, scenes and stage, singing as they go,
Talking and walking, dancing and playing airs
On every instrument that man's skill prepares

All through a little machine, run by a wheel;
And electric apparatus he did conceal,
From watching eyes his invention might steal.
And, there's Marconi, flashing across land and sea
His messages of glad tidings without wires on tree,
Or pole, and nothing to guide his machine,
So far as any one has yet seen.
If such men had appeared in the olden day,
Before Columbus had marked out the way,
They surely would have burned at the stake,
For witchcraft and all for conscience' sake.
Yet with the strides men have made,
With sickle, sword, guns, knife and spade,
With piston, valve, gears, driver and wheel,
Driven by light, electricity, steam and heated steel,
Their thought flying upon the world to reveal
The acts and doings of nature and of man,
From ocean to ocean all over the broad land
And even over the wide extended seas we expand,
With telegraphic cables from land to land,
Bringing all the forces of nature at our command.
With it all, we have made a very little head

Ourselves to control, by designing leaders led.

Those simple rules, by which nature acts,

Might be applied to government its burden to relax,

And take from the shoulders of labor the fearful tax,

To support all the leaches now upon our backs.

Blew Inn

(A Digression)

A sunny Sunday morning in May,
Aimlessly to woods did I stray.
Companions none, but longing to see
One in like plight, I chanced upon three;
The Masons two, wife and man, and one,
A lad in his teens, made up
A quartet with me to fill joy's cup.
With lusty minnows in pail to its fill,
We took up rods and pail, reels and line,
And, in our barque sailed forth to find
Some less wary of the finny kind.
In vain did we tempt the fickle fish;
But at noon instead, with a dainty dish,
Of eggs partly spilled and ham and things
Fit for appetites toil and pleasure brings,
We dined and ate to the brim.

Two shy frogs sitting dreamily on logs
Became prey to us as if native bogs.
Fast flew the flushing day away;
A trolley call, and one and all did say;
Shine on old sol another day.

Courts and Laws

Next our courts and laws come in for review,
Not to gain applause, but my course to pursue.
Laws are rules as is taught in schools
To guide civil conduct into the right,
To redress wrongs and make us keep our plight.
Deeds of a certain kind are called crimes;
For the perpetration of which in historic times,
Men have sought to punish their course to stay,
Every one who does them in some kind of way.
By the power of the state men may collate,
All kinds of acts which by law they state
To be offenses for one them to perpetrate.
These acts in themselves, may be for our good
When understood, yet by the statute they would

Be crimes just the same, whether bad or good.
The original idea of punishment probably grew out
Of our natural impulse just to take a bout
With any fellow who ever did us any dirt
To see if him we could not also hurt
A little more, or just as much as to us he did;
Pull his tooth for our tooth, and his eye with the lid,
For our eye he did black simply to pay him back.
In a later day to give reasons for our laws
Which by the wise were sought, we had to pause,
So then we simply said, punish to stop crime.
Now suppose that I could show that in no time,
Did punishment ever even our crimes diminish,

Much less did it ever bring them to a finish.
Your eyes will open wide when I say to you;
The stopping of crimes punishment will never do.
Men will more chances take, your neck to break,
Your goods to steal, and your girls to snake
Off and defile, even if you are wide awake

Against the whole complicated machinery of the law,
Than they would by getting immediately into your claw;
When with weapons good, you certainly would
Make all respect your rights as you them understood.
The plan indicated above could not all at once
Be put into practice, for you'd be a dunce
To turn loose so many who had never had any
Training in the matter we set up as a crime.
The way for you to do is to drop one at a time
Of your statutory crimes punishable by fine,
Mostly passed to give jobs to a certain class
Of human vegetables who stalk about in brass.
That you may cautiously follow up the scale
In all its detail, and you'll never fail
To accomplish good in giving people their rights
And in keeping them quiet and free from fights.
By the penitentiaries you keep and your jails
Where people sleep with vermin on rails;
Waiting for trial before jury and judge.

Weeks before they are allowed to budge,
Makes them have against you such a grudge;

That when they get loose, as they frequently do

They go at their old tricks with energy anew

To see how dastardly they can act in the crimes they do.

In your hatcheries of crime, the bunch you have to feed

Seems to be increasing with a gradual, steady speed.

The time may come when the gang in the walls,

May outnumber us when at their leader's calls,

They might break out with a united band,

Overpower us, and devastate the land.

So that whatever you do, make your crimes few;

And those you do define, stand firmly to.

The more laws you have the more it'll take

To handle all those who their behests break.

"Laws are a necessary evil" was truly said

By a great hero, now sleeping among the dead.

So the less of this evil upon ourselves we fix

The more good we can with our liberty mix.

Those progressives of you who make such ado

About our laws, and the courts in which you sue,

Want to fill our statutes all the way through

With every law and sumptuary regulation,

On every subject in the whole creation,

That, in their wrought up imagination,

They can conceive of to make litigation;

(Telling us that they comprehend the situation)

They'd put on the books without investigation.

You'd like to snake all this through,

Thinking that nobody is watching you;

But you had better try and hold yourself back;
We are watching you, and I am now on your track.
Now the courts are made the laws to enforce;
It is their job, and you and I of course,
Cannot dictate to them what laws to enforce.
To criticise the courts as the newspapers do
Might put us in contempt, the same as you
In some cases where you had to keep out of view;
Or run a lively race to keep yourself out of jail
By hanging on to some big lawyer's coat-tail.

About your courts I will simply suggest
That whatever might be done I deem it best
Of the things we might do, get judges true,
Learned and wise, and who do not know you
Nor me, nor any of the folks that sue
Their cases in court before them;
The opinions they write with type or pen
Will be free from the bias of men then.
They will consider the laws, sort out the flaws
In each case, and every litigated cause;
So that the judgment they shall render
Making you your supposed rights surrender
Will be honest, no matter what we tender;
Although you practically sink by their blunder
Until in amazement you begin to wonder
Whether your lawyer really did plunder
Through all the books to get you from under

The load that is imposed when your case is closed
In the court of the judge you supposed
Had sense enough not to be bulldozed.

✠ ✠

A Fable—Two Frogs

Two little frogs their legs began to turn,
Haply leaped and jumped into a churn.
The churn was filled about half full
Of milk from which we our butter pull.
One frog to his mate did say:—
"We're here to stay and can't get away.
Now you may paddle and your head addle,
But I'll bebobdaddle if I'll saddle
On myself the task to get out of the flask,
I'm going to die, and no use to cry,
So good-bye," and down he went dead.
The other made no reply, but paddled ahead
And paid no heed to what the first had said.
By and by a big chunk of butter came
And, upon the same froggie rode
Feeling the load off his mind throw'd.
In a short time there came a grunting swine
Walking slowly up out of his grime,
And shaking off his slime, rooted the churn over,
Letting little froggie jump in clover.

Socialism

Nearly all of the animals go in herds,
Fishes, mammals, bees, ants, and even birds.
The snakes are not so socially inclined;

They had rather with none combined,
Slip cautiously alone and snap from behind.
Man has always a social animal been,
To get his food and commit his sin.
He has always stood for organizations,
Municipalities, states and corporations,
Made to protect him against depredations.
Whenever new thoughts take form in his head,
He is sure to try to have others into them led,
By his talks and whatever by him is said.
Man has made laws and written them down,
Telling the good people all not frown;
That by their consent these laws are made:
"The consent of the governed,"
Is exactly what they said.
That is true as the law-makers by your vote,
Are elected your welfare to promote.
Laws are rules laid down for our control,
Pointing out paths where we may not stroll,
Marking the lines in which our rights are defined,
Commanding and forbidding the multifarious kind
Of the things we must do or leave behind.
Some laws are on natural justice based;
That might be speculatively traced

To the dealings of man in his beginning;
Starting out in the races he was winning

Over his ancestors, those animals called "low,"
He might have come upon one not so slow;
Who singly could not be brought down with a blow;
So with his likes he combined the swift one to get
For their food, and their appetites to whet.
Now when this animal combined they took,
The question was up, and not a law book,
By which to decide who should take the hide;
And into what and how many parts the rest to divide:
So they naturally counted the number of their gang,
While this juicy meat did before them hang;
And number parts equal to the number of them
Was equally cut off the beast from stern to stem:
The meat thus divided the hide could not
Be usefully carved up, so they gambled for it by lot:
In the hand of each a pebble to throw at a spot,
They took to try who closest to the mark got;
And the one it who did the nearest hit,
Took away the hide for his skill and grit.
The idea of justice thus received

Is about as good as has ever been achieved,
By reading all the books in every case
Where the law is defined for the human race.
Life might be likened to a game of chance
And the laws, the rules by which we advance

Our men upon the board or throw the lance:
When people together their business transact,
Follow the rules, and courts will solve the contract.
When our forefathers made this Republic of ours,
They established a constitution limiting the powers,
That the government itself could exercise
The best to preserve our liberty they could devise.
Even before this fundamental law they did make,
Which of necessity did part of our liberty take,
They prefaced all our laws for me and you
With certain inalienable rights kept in view:
"That all men were created equal," they knew;
"That life, liberty, and the pursuit of happiness,"
Were set out in plain view, our land to bless.

Now every law since that date passed by the state,
To that extent our liberties infringe, even though we scringe;
And feel the distress, without redress,
Of many iniquitous acts, even by Congress.
If men were actually well-behaved,
Much useless trouble and expense could be saved:
Laws being hobbies our liberties to restrain;
Some barely holding us, even with tight rein.
The socialist man, if I do not mistake,
Would all restraint from our law makers take,
So that the state might feed and regulate
All the peoples who come within its gate,
And all others' properties appropriate,
To the general good as by them understood.

The titles to your lands and everything good
That on them stands, they would concentrate
Into public hands whom they would nominate.
The labor and the work, the leaders would shirk,
Would be done by some one or his clerk.
So that we all would have a good time,
In our day, should we adopt their line.

"Every man has a right to work and eat";
And such clap trap of verbiage we meet,
On every hand as we go over our land.
They jabber, but their sense I can't see.
How can this come in the land of the free?
They produce arguments hoary with age,
Used by many a high-class sage,
That the ownership of property—especially land,
Never had a foundation on which it could stand.
That the whole idea was a fiction once,
And not to see it now one is a dunce.
That all your vested rights on paper,
Are unsound, no matter what caper
Folks may cut their supposed rights to hold,
With all their power and hoarded gold.
If they can unite the working man on their side,
They hope into power to gloriously slide.
The men who labor with their hands have all
United into bands.
Feeling that the little work there is to do
Must pay the most to the ones who pursue

Trades of all kinds and of every hue.
That the work for men to do with hands
Is constant, regardless of supply and demands;
Never once observing that the cost
Of production many jobs them have lost.

So even if they do get more out of that they do;
The valuable time lost in the trades they pursue,
Will more than compensate for th' advanced rate
They obtain from the fewer jobs that remain.
Why it does not occur to them while they dream
What a big world this is with all its demesne,
Is a matter beyond explanation by what I ween.
That work is not confined on this big earth,
But spreads out to give us all a wide berth.
Against trusts and monied corporations,
Men in their stations might form associations
Their rights to demand and their wrongs to reduce,
But against th' individual there is no excuse,
Why unions upon him should heap their abuse.
If one build a house to cover up his head,
Why should union labor try to kill him dead,
By making the cost so high that none can buy,
Houses building now far and nigh.

But all these perplexing questions are upon us;
And the merits and demerits we must discuss,
If practical socialism must come,
We must face it, each and every one.

By the brotherhood of man, maybe we can
Find a way to harmonize every tribe and clan
And save this civilization for the good of man.

✠ ✠

The Public

My subject here is simply a term to express
"A somewhat," the nature of which is a guess.
Of the substance contained in the above term,
It seems almost impossible for one to learn,
No image of it in his mind can he conceive,
Reflects the intelligence he'd wish to receive.
What the public looks like or is,
Is more than you can tell or wis.
According to some it's "ideas in th' abstract."
So let us take that for the real fact.
The public does not seem to be you or I

Or anybody else—I'll tell you why;
Whoever or whatever the thing may be,
He, she, or it shoulders blame for you and me,
For wickedness done in his dear name,
And credit for intended good, the same,
In very many cases that men declaim.
If a bunch of grafters wish to float a deal,
Say in baking powder, wheat, or oat meal;
First the public pulse they scientifically feel,
To discover signs of fever germs in foods,
We've been eating, and such other goods
Of the same kinds we've bought all our lives,
And from which others are supporting wives,
And children as they've done all their lives.
Of course their doctor this pulse carefully felt,
And discovered that germ tracks were smelt

In most of the stuff we put in our pelt.
He discovered too that alum would
Dry up the diaphragm if used in food.
Also that certain foods contained sand,
That might get into the public craw, and
Brace them up too much to patriotically vote
For such a pure food law as they'd like to float.
So after their analysis was properly wrote,

They get their pure food law nicely framed up
To suit their scheme and for the people to gulp.
Then their bugle horns they did blare,
And it carried before we were aware.

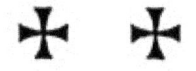

✢ ✢

Physicians

In olden times, doctors and barbers were the same,
As we find in books from which we always gain
Information on all such historic matter.
As bleeding was the thing then to batter
Out diseases the striped pole must be
An emblematic relic of the blood running free
Down and around our hip, thigh and knee.
But the two trades have been now long separated;
And while neither should be underestimated
And both receive their due from me and you,
The barbers' trade is not really and truly due
As much criticism as is the medicine crew.
There are plenty of fine physicians and surgeons,

Who receive their praise from us in legions;
But the "money-rosis" has struck the doctors
As other trades, including divorce proctors.
I well remember in the days long past,
Pulse felt, and a look at the color the tongue cast,
When the doctor was done, and no more was asked.
He said it was simply chills and fever he did believe,
Which a good dose of calomel or blue mass would relieve,
All of which the patient did then and there receive.
You might have had a slight pain in your head,
And you were advised to lie still in bed.
Now call a doctor your wife to see,
And while you sent for only one to fee,
Two or three more and sometimes a score,

To handle the different parts of the sore,
Come in and watch around your door;
Especially if you've got money, and get more.
If you fall and bruise your knee or elbow
A specialist must come to whom they show
Some of the dirt from the place around,
To ascertain if any microbes are found.
If a cough or cold comes in your head,
A sample or two of the sputum that you shed,

Is sealed up and sent away to be analyzed.
They always find 'em, so don't be surprised.
And if plenty of money you can get
To pay all this cost and never sweat,
When your bills at home are all paid,
You'll be then sent off on dress parade.
Doctors never come now and find you well;
Your ailments have names you cannot spell.
And when you ask what you're about to take
The awful malady you have to try to shake
To pronounce its name your jawbone'll break.
As simple a dose as soda and rain water
At the drug store will cost you a quarter.
All diseases now come straight from bacilli
Seen through those microscopes they buy.
Let these germs once your systems fill
You just as well not make your will,
It'll take the farm to pay your doctor bill,
All diseases have now become contagious.

And their catching qualities outrageous.
When you walk do not spit on the street,
Lest your saliva infect those you meet.
No trains are allowed to have a drinking cup
In which others drink, lest you swallow up
The other fellow's germs sticking to the glass
Of the family of microbes in the tubercular class.

No comb or brush is found to smooth your hair,
They're prohibited and blacklisted everywhere.
All your water must be thoroughly boiled
And its palatable flavor entirely spoiled,
To slay the ferocious germs in it coiled.
And even the milk from your fat Jersey cow
Should be pasteurized as never before till now.
We might run down the whole category
Till you were tired, and I get hoary,
But these very things are the doctor's glory.
Of course they are trying to lengthen life's span,
And I'm not going to censure them if I can,
Only caution them to be easy as they can.
They don't catch me often, my father was a physician,
And before he died, he made it his mission
To post me and make me wise on this score.
I have sometimes felt peevish and sore
Because father was too honest to lay up a store
For me to spend when I life began;
My father was above all an honest man.
Once my wife took pneumonic cough

And we for a doctor sent right off.
He came and found genuine bacilli.
Scared me, and made the wife almost cry.
They analyzed, criticised and diagnosed

And sent her away, with my house closed;
And for nights I scarcely dozed.
They gave her just six months of life
Before consumption would part me and my wife.
My plucky woman partly believed what they said,
And moped around a while and stayed in bed.
I had some doubts about what the specialists said,
And relied a little on what an old friend read,
Who had much practical experience, she said.
Of course my doubts about science I hate to tell,
But in a few weeks the wife was entirely well.
If the doctor wants to, let him tell
Why into the aforesaid mistake he fell.
Now you had all better beware and treat us fair,
If you have doubts about what our troubles are
Just do your best, and let nature do the rest.

✠ ✠

Theologians

For the preacher's trade one should have a call,
As has been said concerning the apostle Paul;
Who with power armed with writs to haul
Before magistrates Christians one and all,
And lodge them in jails subject to call
To be prosecuted in the name of the state
For sayings of Christ they did relate.
"Why persecutest thou me?" the Master said;
Then Saul, afterwards Paul, fell as one dead.
When he came to be had a call to preach,
So he went forth all nations to teach.
Not many of you preachers ever had a call,
Nor down as dead did any of you ever fall.
Most of you took to preaching to have something to do,
Although the picking is getting short for some of you,
If the newspaper accounts I'm reading be true.
When the lawyer's job in the country gets short,
He adds insurance, abstracts, and things of that sort;
But when the preacher's picking isn't very good

He'd have ice-cream suppers whenever he could;
Or even quiltings and sewing society aid,
Eked out with dinners and sale of lemonade.
I notice now you're going to take course
In farming to teach the brethren of the rural force;
But I'm afraid that if you begin shoot'n off your head
To some of those old rustics to help earn your bread,
You might get a set'n back worse than Old Ned,

Or even than Saul got when he fell as dead.
Farmers have ideas of their own they've tried;
And wouldn't listen to the pastor or turn aside,
For his book learning he had himself supplied
While off at college that had never been tried.
You might do better holding to the plow,
While your brother farmer was milking his cow,
Feeding his stock and chopping his wood,
And in that way would do him more good.
But the best way for all is to wait for this call.
And don't be in a hurry to be preachers at all.

If you wait a real call to actually hear,
You'll be working soon and will not have to fear,
Without any other call than nature gives
To every animal that on earth now lives;
To be up and doing his fellow man to bless,
Which while doing you'll keep from distress.

✠ ✠

Lawyers

To attorneys, advocates, and counsellors all,
I'm not afraid to speak to you about your call;
Not afraid to give advice, I'm one of you,
You may heed, or I don't care what you do.
You give advice and charge for the same;
Mine I freely give, and you get the gain.
When you get free what to others you sell,
You've something to brag about and tell.
I like you, you bunch of jolly good fellows,
Though you sometimes lunch like Col. Sellers.
And your Sunday suit gets so slick,
That a fly cannot walk on it and stick.
You too are letting people into your trade.
Deeds and legal papers are so easily made,
By real estate agents filling out blanks
Those you write are paid for in thanks.

You sit in your office with high-propped feet,
Longing for a friend to invite you out to eat,
Or waiting for a client to bring around a fee.
Sometimes you read or skip around in glee,
To make the impression that your mind is free;
And that you have plenty of work to do;
And never for a moment take a solemn view
Of how fast business is flying away from you.
Some of you are learning on a motor cycle to ride,
So when an accident occurs you are by the side
Of the injured one to get a damage suit

Against the company whose coffers you'd loot.
Some of you join the gang and get in politics,
To get some legal job they may help you fix.
One of you stirs up strife against divorce,
And gets to be proctor on the welfare force,
And gets a small salary as a matter of course.
Some get to be orators public affairs to discuss.
And get the press over you to make a fuss;
In that way you advertise your brains good

To swing a big case and get a livelihood.
Some join with unions to fight against the trusts,
Others against the unions sling their deadly thrusts.
Thus in battle array, some right and some wrong,
We manage in some way to push ourselves along.
The race of the old-time lawyers is nearly extinct
To whose memory my fond thoughts are linked.
I know a few whose names I'll not give to you
Owing to my plan I intend to follow through,
Not to give names unless to represent a crew.
You know some yourself not in the law for pelf;
I'm one myself if into my record you care to look,
If I hadn't been I need not have written a book
To make a little stake to put away for a rainy day.
Lawyers are not dishonest, no matter what you say,
Except when they serve you to get their pay.

They have to be deceiving to keep up with you:
You will not take your case you wish to sue

To some attorney who could not stand for you.
You know the attorney stands in your place,
And to an honest one you dare not show your face.
I've known lawyers who courted the name of crook,
Merely to catch grafters on their own hook.
You know well when you are sued that you choose
An attorney who will by any ruse, you excuse
To the jury who tried your case for the deeds,
You did, and you know you did not get your meeds.
So shut up your mouth and hie yourself home;
The subject of judges and lawyers leave alone.
Lawyers have always been pillars of the state
To uphold our institutions you'd annihilate.
Their trade is not alone on paper made;
It comes from growth by development's aid.
It's the garnered experience of all the ages,
Written in books upon numberless pages.
It has stood when empires fell,

When to the despots they did loudly tell
Of justice upon him the law'd compel;
It has stood against strife, slaughter and blood,
When other trades and institutions never could;
It rises in the right, iniquity to fight,
To protect the weak against men of might,
Over widows and orphans its protecting arm
Is extended to save the mortgaged farm;
It shields the criminal against the crazy mob

Giving him a trial of which they'd him rob.

For peace and order and justice in the land

Let us ever as true lawyers stand.

✠ ✠

Names

By the use of names we designate
Some particular thing, person or state.
The naming of animals in the first place,
Was put upon Adam as father of the race.
This job imposed upon him no great task,
Because no one's permission he had to ask,
Whether the name suited mule or cow,
Or the name horse he might to kid allow.
Now the names of animals who came
Before him in a long-extended train,

They had to take those which for them he did book
Because they did not have a list over which to look.
All proper names men can find,
Have been so often used by men of their kind,
That when a child is about to be born,
Into the world, the name it shall adorn
Has to be taken from the long list
Of those gone before, or who still persist.
Although we have quite a long catalogue,
We still have to search and our memory jog
To ascertain the character of the ones
Who bore the name about to be given to our sons;
Because any name may have been soiled
By its owner around whom might be coiled
The evidence of some offense the name to suffuse
Before the time we it did choose.
The likes and dislikes for names we take,

Come mostly from the character of the namesake.
A lot of names might be brought to view:
Like Jennie, Sallie, Mollie, Kate and Sue;
Or Perkins, Phelps, Pickering, and Penn,
And a whole book full of names for women and men.
The others need not here be enrolled,
In this little volume, or by me polled.

The things that did once make names great
Generally were acts done for the state,
Mostly in war, e. g., Alexander the Great,
Or Caesar, or even Napoleon the Sedate.
Sometimes names receive much eclat
At home, as well as near and far,
Like Washington, or our Jefferson,
And also Cleveland and Lincoln,
By statesmanship with head and brain
For the public good when peace did reign.
There used to be a time, now almost past,
When patriotism was then in full blast,
That men would sometimes almost actually do things
With no other pay than the consolation it brings,
Simply to be esteemed just, good and true,
With no other motive than to bless me and you.
But now of late men look upon the state
Simply as a fat goose for them down,
As o'er them her wings may spread around,
To hover and her blessings bring down.
The offices men fill to uphold the law,

Or collect our revenues to fat their maw
Are held mostly by ones we did not choose,
Who with politicians by some sharp ruse
Got nominated and elected against our views;
And when elected frame up bills
For legislation that their own pocket fills,

Regardless of the trouble and all the ills,
That fall upon the public that foots the bills.
New bureaus are made about everything
To which a gang of leaches can cling;
With their matrons, clerks and superintendents,
All hangers-on and their bunch of dependents,
Disgracing all over our broad land,
On every hand, the very name of man:
I fear that our present civilization cannot stand,
To live down the iniquity by them thus began.
The euphonious name of Guggenheimer,
Sipniski, Schradski, or even Joe Reimer,
Now is fine if their amounts in bank,
Stood their drafts and never shrank
Below the balance they had on hand
With the banks throughout the land.
A good name is appraised above riches,
But to keep that good to which one hitches,
When anyone can claim any name he likes
And ruin it forever, when off he hikes
To Canada or Old Mexico to get away
From the crimes he did in his day;

Making the name disgraceful he wears,
And none of the same name spares
From sharing the shame brought on the name,
To us, innocent and free from blame,

Except for the acts he did against our name.
Ambition leads us to attempt undying fame,
That after we are dead and in our grave
Our name shall live that we did engrave
Among the world's heroes on every page
Of history that dies not with old age.
But everything to make us famous or great
Has been by someone, somewhere in every state
Of civilization accomplished and achieved,
So no chance is left for us, though grieved.
So let us not try to make our names great;
But instead, unite to rescue our own state,
From the clutches of the vultures at its heart;
And if we succeed at that, when we depart,
Those left behind will bear us in mind,
And write our names in the highest place they find.

✠ ✠

Universal Peace

In all the past the records are full of war;
Men had one desire to be in a continual jar;
Or else the peaceful victories they did win
Were not such as they wrote therein.
Each nation, tribe, and men of ancient race
For each other had nothing but hatred and menace.

Upon the boundaries and rights of each,
The other did recklessly go to reach,
With rapine and murder in their hearts,
To snatch from each other all such parts
Of their lands, and their goods to confiscate,
As could be done by the hordes they did aggregate.
Their warriors and men to subjugate,
Their women and fair maids to subject
To brutality, and any other object
As they chose upon them to impose.
There were only two kinds in those times
Of peoples on earth, those in their own confines,
And barbarians who dwelt anywhere else,
Regardless of who they were, Goths, Huns or Celts.
No tie of sympathy was known or recognized,
Between those different tribes;
Each for the other was lawful prize.
Robbery, theft, and murder were terms,
Applied to deeds committed at home;
These same acts out where they did roam,
Were designated bravery and prowess,

When upon barbarians they did egress,
With battle-axe, darts, helmet and shield,
Bent on the slaughter of their fellow man;
For conquest and glory, they led the van;
Over mountains filled with perpetual snow,

Into heated valleys where the sun did glow;
They fought for pride, religion and show;
As upon crowned heads they wore
Laurels of victory for blood and gore.
But now has dawned a better day;
From ocean to ocean where men survey
Their lands and the boundaries fix
Where rights of each the line restricts;
And treaties with one nation is made
With others to settle their commerce and trade.
They bring across oceans in merchant marine,
Luxuries of life now by us all seen,
Grown and shipped from the uttermost lands,
Divided from us by seas, deserts and sands.
Those natural laws we are learning to use,
Based upon justice according to the views
Of publicists and statesmen applied
To nations dealing with nations the world wide.
Now the crude implements of death once used
By ancients, are thrown aside and refused.
In place of triremes propelled by oars,
Steel-clad battleships ride by scores,
Manned with guns throwing missiles miles;

Around our coasts and adjacent isles;

Our barricades and our battlements,

Our field glasses and our armaments;

Our powder in guns and in mines,

With deadly explosives of all kinds,

Making killing a thing of skill

Upon the thousands our inventions kill,

All are bringing war to a standstill.

No longer do we hand to hand in war engage;

Foes rushing foes with eyes in a rage;

Instead, the scientific gunner his aim to gauge,

Miles away, his gun adjusting to suit,

Deals death to thousands, wherever he may shoot;

With no malice in his heart, by electric touch,

Some mine is exploded, killing and destroying as much

In a single blow, as was done in a day the old way;

And in all the soldiers are out of the fray.

Why should we slaughter and fellow men slay,

In this unimpassioned, calculating, scientific way?

If such things, done by the whole nation,

Were done by one, it'd be murder in our estimation.

Inventions and knowledge lead towards peace;

And the frequency of war decrease;

The more we know of our fellowman.

The less we like to cut off his span.

So let the dove of peace hover over the globe,

And in humanity's cause we ourselves enrobe;

Till from war and all its sickening pall,
We advance, and universal peace install;
And we may, unless we get up a protocol,
Over which we may fight to see who is right,
In the interpretation thereof withal.

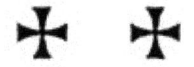

☥ ☥

Music

About the subject of music what can I say?
That mystical combination we sing and play?
The origin of which none seem to know;
For as far back into the past as we can go,
From the time that Circe and her maids,
In their lonely isle of forests and glades,
Their magic spells, in song, upon the sailor wrought,
With all his crew, to their abode they brought,
To change them to swine from the forms of men;
Until wise Ulysses, by some godlike ken,
Undid the deed done his men confined in a pen;

Or when Orpheus with his lyre in his hand,
Held his sway through th' enchanted land.
So 'twould be a waste of valuable time,
The history and origin of music to put into rhyme.
It seems that it has long over us held sway;
Back from the long ago to the present day.
But in all times before this day of ours,
When men have harnessed th' unseen powers:
It did take the skill of finger tips
Or the trill of throat and puckered lips,
To wake from vibrations thereby made,
The thrilling chant and sweet serenade.
But now with pricking pins of steel,
Those same vibrations come from turn of wheel,
When in dents lightly made on a disc,
Which around and around we playfully whisk;

The pin points strike in and then out,
As the thing is whirled about;
And, by magnifying the scratching it makes
The picture of the whole sound action it takes;
And reproduces the vibrations on our ear,
Of an opera or any piece we wish to hear.
By the numerous machines by inventors made,
The sweet music once by human skill played,

Has passed into commerce of daily trade.
For a few dollars one can buy,
A music maker if he will but try.
Although the music thus made is not the real thing;
Yet instruments are designed that give it the ring.
True music that really stirs the hearts of men
That comes from the masters with the pen,
Must be by human skill played,
As ever behind its dress parade,
Stands the soul of the master, flowing with the sound,
As it comes to our ears in tones profound,
Or tintinnabulations of drum or fife,
Calling us to war and its deadly strife;
Or those mysterious strains of the violin,
In the hands of the artist held in,
By his neck, hands, shoulders and chin
So none can tell where he stops for fiddle to begin;
Both moving together in such perfect time
As we sit in rapture, listening to the chime.
Will ever the sense of music in man,

Having remained since history began,
Be obliterated in time to come;
And his taste for sounds become numb,
By the strain on him these machines make,
Hounding him by their grating sleep or wake,

By the screeching buzzes they make;
With our songs all ground up into rag,
Even the stirring ones of the glorious flag,
And those sedate hymns sang in church
Which ragtime has sought to besmirch.
But of all of this let us not complain,
Even if we lose our desire for the grand refrain;
Maybe some time the genius of the great,
Will some better sense create,
For its loss fully to compensate.

✠ ✠

Painting and Art

When I think over the subject of painting and art
Nothing occurs new that to you I can impart
Which might bring reformation in the way
These subjects could be treated in our day.
The men of ancient times, with keen vision,
Bent over canvas and marble with a precision
Not equalled or surpassed, marking lines of light
And shades, bringing life and nature into full sight,
Throwing upon cloth the earth and beclouded sky.

With its valleys green and mountains high,
Divided into parts with ever-widening and winding streams,
Their shores lined with foliage green and rocks in seams;
And scraggy trees, as through them the moonbeams
Throw their mild and mellow light in shimmering sheen;
And fading lines of landscape merging into sky,
With its diversified colors upon our watching eye;
And from the dead, cold marble stand out
The forms of women and men showing their features and clout,
Bringing out every expression of muscle and face,
Revealing the thoughts and passions in lines they trace
Of all the joys of life and the agonizing look,
Even to portraying the dying groan one undertook.
To show up nature is the whole object of art;
To make the scenes natural and life impart.
Now our skill in inventions throwing light,
We absolutely copy nature and bring it out right.
Men with their skill and labor bringing out a view,

With tinsel and touch to give it the correct hue,
Cannot come up to daguerreotype or kodak
In throwing out the front or showing up the back.
Thus onward our wheels of progress are rolling,
Crushing out the heart of Genius strolling
Over lands vying, with his puny hands,
With forces of nature invention commands.
We should pause sometimes in our rapid flight,
Long enough to reflect on the dangers that might
Wreck our civilization; children would their lives destroy
Were they allowed to handle guns as a toy;
So with man in his audacious daring
Handling these forces recklessly, caring
Little for those who are smashed beneath their grinding,
As the end to the glories of art they are finding.

✠ ✠

My Fiddle

When my years numbered less than ten,
I stayed with an uncle and aunt now and then,
Who lived a few miles from our own door.

Now when I think of those days of yore,
When I lingered around the cabin door,
In rapture listening to the violin,
Held under our old black man's chin;
And its melody did my young heart win,
Recollection goes back to my violin.
This old fiddle came to me in a trade,
That I with our work-hand made;
And I learned to play for the serenade.
I rosined my bow and handled it too,
And loved this fiddle the whole day through.
I played it nights before I went to sleep;
Rolled it in flannel its tone to keep;
Put it in the box which I did make;
And took it out mornings soon as I'd wake.
My aunt, who lived at the house where I went,
With whom I stayed and many hours spent
Was of the old school in the ideas she had;
The most things I thought good she deemed bad.
A deck of cards would have made her collapse;
And for amusements now offered chaps,
They'd been abomination in her very sight;
The fiddle she thought her soul would blight.
And even the box it was carried in,

Was contaminated with the ghost of the violin.

This vile thing was played for the dance,
And that made it the horror of my aunt's.
Of all this I was then in ignorant bliss.
So feeling good, I did not want to miss
The chance to show my aunt how I did play
On my fine instrument with much display.
So carefully boxing it up, I took it to stay
At the home of my aunt, to whom I'd show
My performance with the fiddle and bow.
When I arrived she greeted me before she did see,
What was under the seat in the buggy with me.
When I pulled it out I plainly saw
A cloud come over her as she stood in awe.
She did not at that time speak her full mind
But in memory lingering now I find
She said to herself something or other
To the effect that my father and mother,
Who were her sister, and in law her brother,
Didn't have the same care for their child,
As she did for hers, or else how could they defile
A little boy like me with such a tool of evil
Specially devoted to sin and the service of the devil.
I took my poor fiddle and lugged it to my room,
Where I did not string it up so very soon.
But on one rainy day I took it out to play
Strains of old hymns that in my memory lay.

The thunder's crash and the lightning's play
Could not from my aunt keep away
The penetrating sound my violin bore,
Only a moment and she was at my door.
I saw in horror my aunt stand before,
With uplifted hands as her eyes bore,
Riveting me in silence to the floor.
The anger, pity, grief, fear and pain
In her face made upon me its lasting stain.
In words not spoken as much as shrieked,
She revealed why her face was streaked
With the lines I saw when she appeared:
"Put that horrid thing away," she whispered;
"Put it in the back closet and lock the door."
She insisted: "Hide it quick, I implore;
The Lord in his wrath will blow the house o'er!
Don't you know better than to tempt God in that way,
While the lightning and thunder His power display?"
I admit that I did not know, but in my heart,
Then tender in years, was lodged a dart
It took years to remove; even now when I start
Upon my new violin some music to play
I wonder sometimes if in some mysterious way

There is not lurking in it some demon still,
Its tones and notes sound so awfully shrill.
I would not for a single moment profane
The memory of my dear aunt I still retain,
Nor at her sincere beliefs cast one single slur.

I write here what did actually occur.

A coolness between me and the fiddle I love

Sprang up from the incident related above,

That lasted all the days of my youth

When I might have learned the violin in truth;

That instrument none can ever master,

Who does not cling to it in every disaster.

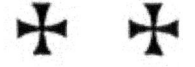

✠ ✠

Scientific Ethics

Having now had with you our several quarrels
We advance our lance to the subject of morals.
Ethics is a theme from which I can glean
Some substantial hopes for a better day;
When, with our prejudices all put away,
We shall all learn to act and think the things,
Which keep in view the good life to us brings.

While this subject is as plain as a b c
The same for some reason you fail to see.
Morals are the manners and customs one adopts
For himself in private life, while he hops,
Or walks and talks with his fellow men.
Good morals are good habits and bad, bad.
Habits are easily made, and when once had,
They are hard to break for anybody's sake.
The "stream of thought" seems the road to take,
Where it once had run anywhere under the sun.
Morals are the acts of which life is composed
That we have upon ourselves imposed.
This definition was made by Immanuel Kant,
But as it is self evident, he needn't want,
All the credit to claim if I use the same.
Laws cause you do as others compel you;
Ethics cause you to do what you like to.
There are only two things that push us along.
Think about it till you rack your brains,
And you'll find them always pleasures and pains.

Some even take pleasure in their sorrow and grief;
And you'd not be thanked for offering a relief;

Nor for producing a balm to heal their wounds,
From which they suffered, regardless of their grounds.
Men, of their humility have been so proud;
That lugubriously, they'd stand up in any crowd;
Or with their heads bowed and on bended knees,
With the pride of their humbleness you they'd freeze.
The pleasures we desire and the pains we shun,
Were our only motives since the world begun.
Now keep this in mind as its use you'll find,
As we treat of ethics and its motives behind.
"Self-imposed precepts" are not the moral code,
Prevalent in places where men their guns load,
To meet a fellow man in the public road,
To try out the question with bullets of lead,
On the field of honor, till one or both are dead;
Nor is it the legal code enacted by man,
Making rules against things under ban.
Morals deal with acts men actually intend,
Those motions adapted to some end.
"The wild gesticulations of a lunatic,"
Or of a crazy man who automatically throws a brick,

Bear no relation to the discussion of ethics.
The standards of morals take their hue
From the aims of life men hold in view.
The pessimist says life's a failure entire,

So to meet the demands his views require,
A scheme of acts adapted to shortening life
To get this set soonest out of the strife,
And all the sad and tragic things,
The whole of existence to them brings,
Would be the highest standard of acts,
Which in goodness one for them enacts.
The optimist takes a very different view,
Life's a pleasure while he its joys pursue.
For him a general life suited to make,
Life long, broad and deep for his sake,
Would be a good banner at him to shake.
So we say, bad morals are bad, and good, good.
The reason the subject by you is not understood,
Is, that while you must surely know,
You constantly misapply to ethics one word as you go.
The meaning of this word if you don't get,
Is from stupidity, for you never yet
Went into a store anything to buy or even try,
But a practical demonstration was before your eye.
The first thing you ask about a razor or knife,

Is this, "Is it good?" and the clerk doesn't cry,
"What do you mean!" if he wants you to buy.
He politely answers, "Both these tools cut good,
As they are warranted, one whiskers, and one wood,
And both of them do their part very good."
If one of you farmers wished to acquire a cow,
You wouldn't ask whether she could make a bow;

You would enquire how much milk she gave,
And how much butter, and could she save
You some expense in the way she'd behave.
If such questions had all been left out,
And the seller had known what he was about,
He'd said, "She's good," and everything's understood.
If a female reader went to buy a new spring hat,
And the thing was in style, you would close your chat.
If it was in style, it's good, every fool knows that,
The bargain's made and the hat charged to pap.
The same thing is true of skirts and hoops,

Of dogs and cats, and chickens in coops;
You can't look about or run around,
Without understanding this word always so profound,
And mysterious when applied to my theme;
With yawning face you almost dream,
And look confused when I try to tell what I mean.
You never ask about any of the things I've spoke,
Whether they say their prayers and never joke,
To speak of such, you at me your fun poke.
Now we'll see whether you are sensible folk,
When you try to shed your customary cloak
Of prejudice and mysticism you croak,
Every time you try sense to ethics to apply.
Common sense teaches us there is no reason why,
The definition will not fit conduct every whit,
As it did other things about which I've writ.
Conduct is good if its ends come through,

And its natural results are good for me and you.
I take the optimist's view, life's a blessing,
And when to you my words I'm addressing,
Say whether I'm right in possessing,
The notion that acts are morally right and good,

That contribute to life as above understood.
In its thickness, breadth and length, all those things,
Which happiness achieve, diminishing man's stings.
Before us examples have been set by teachers,
By Immanuel Kant better than preachers;
That each one of our actions should lofty be,
That each would be a model for a code of morality.
This form of hedonism I would gladly place
Before the eyes of the whole human race.
Asceticism is a term derived from the Greek,
Applied to monks, signifying the exercises they seek,
By which they distinguish themselves in that they do,
For favor with the deity in the lines they pursue,
Away from their fellow man as much as they can.
Virtue is a term originally meaning prowess,
And as applied to bravery they did possess;
It aroused the ancients to courage in distress.
When the Old Bard sang "the wrath
Of Peleus' son against those in his path;

When his armies did advance with spear and lance,
Against the Trojans against whom he did advance;
Or of him sulking in his tent, nursing his spleen

Against tall Agamemnon for acts in being mean
Towards him in regard to a captive maid
Upon whom he had his affections laid."
And all the bloody deeds done by gods and men,
Breathing anger from their nostrils when
Upon each other their darts they did hurl,
And in the dust many bleeding bodies did curl;
As these savage men struggled for their prize;
To their gods whole hecatombs did they sacrifice
Of poor dumb brutes that could not sympathize
With them in their bloody wars and heroic cries.
Out of virtue as thus defined did arise
Asceticism and all the horrid tortures it did devise.
Even now men are so wedded to their inspired books
And things written in them by ancients where one looks

To find every act for you and me so well defined
That they claim that all experience combined,
Cannot those precepts change to suit the age;
Although we point out inconsistency on every page.
They even allege that what by their book is said,
Makes things good or bad under each particular head.
That even as simple a thing as theft,
If out of their book the subject were left,
There would be nothing in our practical observation
To distinguish whether or not stealing was a proper avocation.
Whatever of man's moral nature the origin may be,
Whether he was created with a certain propensity,
Or whether our tendencies are a matter of growth;

One thing is certain, and needs not any oath,
To prove that our several tastes may be improved,
To treat our fellow man as it him behoved;
And toward ourselves the truer to be,
Until our standards and the right did agree.

If all the acts that you and I must do,
Were written into mandates constantly held in view,
And we should follow them all the way through,
We still would be nothing but very slaves,
Marching under orders of some specially wise knaves.
Now if one in what he does, lives to the very top,
Of his own ideals, him we cannot stop,
Until for him his ideas we raise; he is up to full speed,
For the requirements of all are not if the same meed.
Most of man's motions should be left to his whims,
Whether he rides or walks, or even swims.
Moral conduct being by each self imposed,
The acts men do will naturally be disclosed,
In the things they like in the tastes disclosed.
When the acts of men are ruled by laws enacted,
From the category of ethics they are subtracted.
No human motions should be forced or restrained,
Unless the welfare of others is to be attained.
In some general sense, everything I do,

To a limited extent, has its natural effect on you.
By two meeting in the road, one of us must turn,
To let the other pass or his rig might overturn.

By breathing the air some oxygen I must consume,
Also infecting what remains by what I exhume.
When in the market I buy my daily supplies,
That alone has a tendency to make the price rise;
So that you have to pay more for your store.
Thus in many and varied ways our motions bear
Some natural disadvantages we should all share,
In our relations each with each as we live everywhere.
Any physical fact, however simple it may look,
May change aspect by the turns it took,
Showing how the morality of any motion,
May appear and disappear, simply by the notion
We have about those unseen motives in its track
Preceding, going with, or following it back.
In presence of ladies a man takes off his hat,

To show respect for them and nothing but that.
The morality of this act is not hard to adjust.
The same gentleman to brush away the dust,
Takes off the same hat in perfect disgust.
In each case the taking off the hat was in view.
The one act was moral, while the other it's true,
With the question of ethics had nothing to do.
He now takes off his hat at the command of the law,
In the presence of the court where he waits in awe.
Being tired of the hat, he takes it off to sell,
Now the above illustration you know so well,
That its application I'll leave you to spell.
"Nothing's good or bad but the thinking makes it so."

Behold the beauty of ethics, let us make it grow.
If you want plants to thrive, cultivate the soil,
Don't over fertilize, or you will make them spoil.
We may stimulate our desires for good morals,

And our desire for good deeds, even by quarrels.
We may over stimulate the passions of the youth,
Even when trying upon them to impress the truth.
By unduly stimulating their appetite for gains,
And their desires for pleasures without enduring the pains;
And by excess their natures may be changed.
In that way we destroy their faculty to enjoy,
The real blessings of life born of strife.
Rewards and punishments for acts and omissions,
Are causes for delinquencies and its commissions.
Both have their way their victims to sway,
From the natural paths of right every day.
Every good act brings its consequential pay
And every wrong act its own punishment,
Upon all who upon mischief are always bent.
But to add to the natural consequence of things,
Which their performance usually brings,
This over pay in the nature of rewards,
Drives one on until the pay alone he regards,

And the nature of crimes fades out of view,
While the punishment alone is considered by you.
Thus on we are naturally driven from our path,
Straying out of the right and the pleasures it hath.

Most of our motions should be left open to choice
To develop our selective faculties in acts and voice,
That make us kind and fellows to rejoice.
A certain kind of approval we feel,
That might be compared to the scent flowers yield,
Upon the doing or even contemplation of acts.
There is also a stifling sensation coming about,
The doing of things about which there is a doubt,
As to whether we ought, although never found out,
Think, do, or pursue the thing we're about.
Conscience is the name applied
To this moving feeling with our faculties allied.
And some say it is a true moral guide.
But experience finds conscience in this plight,
It approves everything we think to be right,

And condemns all things in our sight,
That even from ignorance we deem wrong that may be right.
For conscience' sake many have been burned at the stake,
To appease its gnawings, and thirst for blood to slake.
Gored by its pricks, Hindu mothers, their own babes,
In innocence swathed, into the seething waves,
Of the River Ganges, writhing, religiously they fling,
While to this river god their hymns they sing,
Galled by conscience the monk and anchorite,
In dark caves, out of human sight,
Tear their flesh and do themselves every spite
To humiliate themselves in heaven's sight.
What a freak conscience has proved to be,

Is illustrated in a story by Heinrich Heine,
Of a certain judge in a certain state,
Having condemned eight hundred by his mandate,
To be burned at the stake for witchcraft,
One day conscience threw at him its own shaft.
He imagined too that he was guilty of the crime,

That so many others had been during his time.
So to quiet his conscience he paid the fine;
And having declared himself guilty, did resign,
And purge his soul in punishment condign.
Conscience may help us our morals to regulate,
But first of all, we must our conscience educate,
By educating the head by which it is led.
Know the right and do it too as best you can
And conscience will aid you to be a man.
To learn the right, and it pursue,
Read all books and observe the actions of man,
Acquire by your own experience all you can;
Value conduct as you would value your goods,
Digest the subject as you do your foods,
Always keeping in view that present good,
Is often best achieved, when understood,
By enduring pains now to prepare us for pleasures,
In the days to come in greater measures.
After all, the art which makes life a success
In blessing those we love to bless,
Is to find th' equilibrium of pleasures and pains,

As we do our business losses and gains.
Altruism is a word by Auguste Compte made,
Meaning regard for others, which he truly said,
We should cultivate and human love assimilate.
Sometimes the best thing for others we can do,
Is not to worry them, but our own course pursue,
And to ourselves be true, and they'll pull through.

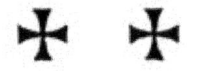

✠ ✠

Sunday Laws

Having enjoyed our quarrels, before we pause,
Let us take a look at your Sunday laws.
In olden time Sabbath breaking was a crime
Of such deep hue, that if anything you do
On that blessed day, even to earn a dime,
By shoveling snow, just about the time,
You begin to know that you must explore
For a little bread to keep wolf from your door.
Now the reason they did pense, for making that offense,
As I divine the most heinous of their time;

Was, that of all the days, it only took six,
For God the funds to raise and no plans to mix,
To build heaven and earth and all stars to fix;
And that the job was all finished so good,
By sundown Saturday night, as they understood,
That on Sunday He had nothing left to do;
So the Lord had to rest, and now must you.
If mistaken in the reasons as to me it looks,
Plenty of Sunday laws are found in your statute books;
And you can read them all yourself,
By taking them off their shelf.
But all those laws have now grown so very old,
And all the pages that them do hold,
Are all stuck together with moss and rust,
So that if you really and truly must,
Take a look at them yourself to see if they are just,
It would be better to hire some old maid or hag,

Who would supply herself with a dust brush and rag
From their pages to scrub away the mold of decay.
Every few years, say one in ten,
Some one or two of our fanatic men,
Or some great big oratorical fellow,

Who imagines that with all ease he can bellow,
And scare the boys their toys to put away,
On the holy, blessed Sabbath day.
As once happened in my own native state,
In almost a comparatively modern date.
This oratorical man became prosecutor of the law;
And he began in earnest to apply his jaw.
He gave us such a jar, that it was hard a cigar,
Or even a loaf of bread to get near or far.
Finally this one did his feathers plume,
And a race for Congress he began to assume;
Thinking that trip he could easily fly.
We then commenced to sing "as in days gone by,"
Before he was walking about our doors stalking,
Upon our heads to precipitate his wrath,
To keep us all in the old straight and narrow path.
In not such an awfully long time, we awoke to find,
That by somebody's nudge, our man was criminal judge.
Dead sure now was he that he could scare all the boys away
From everything that looked like work or even play,

On the Sabbath day, and being in the lurch,
Haply a number would stumble into church,

When the choir began to sing and the coin to ring
In the collection box handed around by a sly fox.
Criminal informations for men in every station,
Who in his estimation, were the Sabbath breaking,
And the church forsaking, issued from his court,
Patiently did the folks go their bails,
And barely kept them out of our jails,
Till the humane change of venue came:
Then alas for his fame, nothing but blame,
For his services lent, and the people's money spent.
By simple non-use laws may die, in the public eye.
When they go out of date, there is no need to legislate;
They are always considered as off the slate.
So let all our captives out with joy and glee,
And let us learn one thing from the Man of Galilee,
That the Sabbath was made for man.

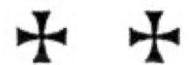

✠ ✠

True Religion

To work and love and live and do
For others as for oneself, in my view,
Would be a good religion for me and for you.
To help ourselves and others to educate,
That all false pride, selfishness and hate,
Come from ignorance and is not innate.
It is born of the admiration some bestow
On fools who parade around to make a show
Of their wealth, and also the clothes they wear,
Thinking themselves too good our company to share.
'Tis not the books we read, nor the speed,
That we travel, nor our boasted creed;
'Tis not the strength we have to believe,
All the tales that from others we receive;
Nor the ugly faces we make when we grieve;
Nor those long drawn out sighs we heave;
Nor even the sorrow we feel for crimes,
Committed away back in ancient times,
By Adam and Eve among their vines
Of the lovely Garden of Eden
Where before there was not a weed in.
Go to church if you please, don your bonnet and hike,
Take a front seat or sit with the choir if you like,

Invite others too, but don't frown if they do
Let you go by yourself if they want you.
When you see a brother come to great grief,

Don't take that chance to give yourself relief,
Of a burden you've carried to get a chance
To heave at him while down, your pious lance;
Put your arms around his neck, his pains to check,
And take some other time his sins to inspect.
Put your money in the missionary field,
To send to all China and all around you feel,
Like saving them from their idols to whom they kneel;
Spread yourself on land and sea to get them in the band;
All this you do and have not charity,
And your religion is not right for me.
Cut out Sunday, sin, satan and hell,
Leave the gods up where they are wont to dwell;
Change all of your songs about heaven above
To things upon our earth and human love;
Put off your mourning, lugubrious whine
And think of man as the one divine;
Learn to talk and walk and act
As if man's freedom was a real fact.

Let your parsons take off their gowns,
And smooth out all their wrinkly frowns;
And preach about potatoes, corn and hay,
Just as if folks on earth intended to stay.
Let deacons and monks and all their crew,
Find work for themselves to toil and do;
Use all your churches, temples and spires,
According to man's natural and ordinary desires;

Stop talking about inspired books and creeds,

But show your faith by human thoughts and deeds.

Immaculate conception and total depravity,

Are entirely too heavy for mortal's gravity;

Baptism, holy unction, and the new birth divine,

Are elements in which gods alone may shine.

All our superstitions and fears and shame,

Originate in reverence for some holy name,

Burned into man by torch, faggot and flame.

Prophets, priests and seers of old,

So long their marvellous tales have told,

That none on earth but the reckless and old,

A doubt against them dare to hold.

Their ancient books and maps and charts,

Are indelibly branded upon our hearts.

From childhood hour at chime of bell

All congregate to hear the preacher tell

Of the garden of Eden where the serpent bold,

To our first mother did his story unfold;

And, that fascinated by that shiny snake,

She has doomed us all to the burning lake,

With no water our scorching thirst to slake.

He tells us too with all his might and main,

That for our crimes the pensive one was slain;

And that by his death on the cruel cross,

We may recoup our first mother's loss.

That all are bound in the chains of sin,

Steeped in iniquity she did begin,

By that headlong fall our mother Eve fell,

And, unless we believe the tales they tell,

Our lot will be cast with the damned in hell.

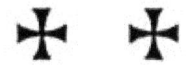

✠ ✠

Immortality

(A Digression.)

When for us our eyes are closed in silent sleep,
And over our rigid body is spread the sheet,
While loved ones around us sob and weep.
When in black our form is shrouded;
And taken to some church all crowded,
Our last rites to receive at loving hands,
Who over our coffin wreathe their garlands

Of flowers, whose fragrance perfume
The air, while loving hearts with song attune,
The stillness to break in hymns of hope;
And the speaker in his talk to cope
With human grief and doubts and fears,
Says consoling words to dry up our tears.
When in our grave, made with pick and spade,
Our embalmed body is solemnly laid;
Does that end us all and all our parade?
Is that all of life to end in dust?
From which our body came once robust?
Or will there come some unseen power
Our lost life to restore in some distant hour,
By some loud trumpet blast us awake
From deep sleep our slumber to break?
Who pines the answer to know,
May have to wait, or the knowledge forego.
Science teaches that what of life we see,
In man as in vegetation, shrub and tree,

Are manifestations of acts the body performs.
That mystic thing called "thought" man's life adorns,
Is but the throbbing of the active brain.
That each lobe and part of the brain,
Responds to particular senses we feel.
One convolution smells, one hears, one sees;
One urges locomotion, or brings us to our knees;

As upon them play the subtle waves from without
Receiving the response within of what we're about.
If all this be true, how can it be
That when this machine is destroyed as we see,
That these results can obtain thus set free.
When the grey matter of the brain is back in dust,
Into its original atoms rudely thrust.
Unless it be that life itself is a thing apart,
And the brain, nerves and throbbing heart,
Are but the instruments through which it plays,
And when this body in which it now stays,
With all of its parts, is dead and gone,
Another new body shall us adorn.
They tell us such things in a book divine;
And that this new body shall shine,
Forever amid the stars and in glory shall walk,
Around a throne and to the king shall talk;
And that under the shade of the tree of life,
Find eternal peace free from toil and strife.

✠ ✠

Death

Death always strikes with a terrific blow,
Because it drives us to where we do not know.
All the saddened past has been filled with a guess.
Ages have been spent in trying to relieve its distress.
Men have sought magic and the spells it casts
To answer questions and all inquiries of death asked.
Yet, after all, we simply know that it is the fate
We all must equally share with those we love or hate.
Life is but a short story for us when it is told;
Its brief animation for the young and for the old
Is only an agitation, a ripple on the waves of time.
A few joys, a few sorrows, a few thoughts sublime
As onward we speed into the Great Beyond unknown.
Could we but open the doors and see the paths strown
With all the remains of the billions before us thrown

Into the gaping jaws of death, devouring its own,
We might then unravel its mysteries deep,
We might then have visions of those who sleep;
But into that vast chasm none are allowed to peep.
Vain it is to pry into this oblivion profound,
Vain to attempt its hidden meaning to expound;
Vain to ask why the hungry jaws of this Monster Great
Does not spare our loved ones, why he should immolate
Kings in palaces and peasants in huts of want,
Babes in cradles and aged ones lean and gaunt.
If we are inevitably doomed to this common end;
Should we fear when towards it our journeys tend?

We cannot shun it by fear or by hope,
We must meet it, and with its pangs must cope.
In which ever way our winding paths may lead
Death faces us with its devastating looks of greed.
It comes to us in a thousand different ways;
It visits us at night when the sun has hid its rays;

It greets us at noonday when the sun is high;
No one can escape its ever-vigilant eye;
All the living must yield up to it and die.
Is death a curse, then all the living are cursed;
Is death a blessing, then all the living will be blessed.
It cannot be an evil, nature creates nothing wrong;
And it is only nature while we follow it along.
Mother earth brings us all into this life;
And this same mother calls us back from its strife.
Can it be that our mother would be unkind?
In a universal mother, universal love we find.
Although her children be numbered by millions;
And all her numberless offspring run into billions;
Yet no partiality she shows; all are treated the same;
Her rules are based on fate, break them and bear the blame.
How could her laws be varied to suit her flock?
Anarchy would reign and destroy her stock.
One universal law; death waits us all;
So let us be courageous while we wait its call.

Milton Keynes UK
Ingram Content Group UK Ltd.
UKHW030910151124
451262UK00006B/851